T0380730

A Little Colored Girl Travels to Another World

Phyllistine Goode Poole

Cover illustration by John Clinzo "Sonny" Goode Jr.

To order additional copies of this book, contact:
Xlibris
844-714-8691
www.Xlibris.com
Orders@Xlibris.com

ISBN: Softcover   979-8-3694-0603-8
        Hardcover   979-8-3694-0604-5
        EBook   979-8-3694-0602-1

Print information available on the last page

Rev. date: 07/22/2024

In memory of librarian Margaret Reid Isbill Achterkirk who founded an integrated public library in Lowell, North Carolina, in the Jim Crow era. This was in the early nineteen sixties. Because of her strong commitment to public service, she created and brought to library patrons and the community innovative and enriching activities such as puppet shows and summer reading programs. She also introduced to many, especially children, classic literature they might not have otherwise known about or read. As one of those children, I remember that she gave us access to and enticed us to read titles Like *Gone with the Wind, His Eye Is on the Sparrow, A Tree Grows in Brooklyn* and *To Kill a Mockingbird* by putting them front and center on a display case near the entrance of the library. Former child patrons, like me, remember Margaret Reid Isbill Achterkirk and testify that because she introduced us to the world of books, we improved academically, did well in school, and "visited" worlds, times and people beyond our small-town environment. Mrs. Achterkirk's influence lives on in us who continue to make the library our house by the side of the road. In our professional and personal lives, we invite others to come in, and we help them discover the wealth of materials and services the library has to offer.

Dedicated to colored girls, especially those I grew up with in Lowell, North Carolina, and surrounding areas.

In appreciation of my Goode family's long-standing friendships with the Crawford, Seigle and Surratt families and my community in Lowell which was like an extended family.

Thank you, L. Seigle and Wilma Ann Worthy for your wonderful commentaries.

"It was the best of times, it was the worst of times…."

-----*Charles Dickens, A Tale of Two Cities*

weather-icon-sun-rain
----*gnokii--Sirko Kemter https:openclipart.org/detail/170680/weather-icon-sun-rain*

I grew up in the nineteen fifties and early sixties and to some was a "little colored" girl."

"Over the past century the standard term for Blacks has shifted from "Colored" to "Negro" to "Black" and now perhaps to "African American."

Changing Racial Labels—-----Tom W. Smith
https://www.jstor.org

Not so very,very,very long ago I grew up on the tail of **Jim Crow**.

crow—-JohnClinzo "Sonny" Goode Jr. author's brother
African American Baby (full-length portrait,wearing christening gown) —-Du Bois,
W.E.B. (William Edward Burghardt),collectorPublic Domain, Library of Congress
http://www.loc.gov/

As a little colored girl, I lived in a **triple** world: the **segregated** world of Jim Crow, a loving family and community world, and the world of books I discovered through an **integrated** library.

And one was a great surprise that opened up my eyes.

But not…

The Jim Crow World

My segregated neighborhood across the track was what is now called "black."

When I got on a city bus, I took a backseat "reserved" for "us," colored people like me, you see.

----Sonny

These are signs of the time:

At a restaurant

A bus station

A **five and dime**

—-*Sonny*

And a Clinic….

with separation of races by hour within it.

Separate health care services and facilities, there were more than a few, including Negro and White hospitals, too.

LALLIE·KEMP·CHARITY·HOSPITAL
CLINIC & CLINIC HOURS
Monday
OB (COLORED) 8:00 A.M. TO 11:00 A.M.
GYN (COLORED) 1:00 P.M. TO 4:00 P.M.
Tuesday
MEDICINE (WHITE) 8:00 A.M. TO 12:00 NOON
PEADIATRICS (WHITE) 1:00 P.M. TO 3:00 P.M.
Wednesday
OB (WHITE) 8:00 A.M. TO 11:00 A.M.
GYN (WHITE) 1:00 P.M. TO 4:00 P.M.
DENTAL (WHITE) 8:00 A.M. TO 12:00 NOON
Thursday
SURGERY (WHITE) 8:00 A.M. TO 12:00 NOON
SURGERY (COLORED) 1:00 P.M. TO 4:00 P.M.
Friday
MEDICINE (COLORED) 8:00 TO 12:00 NOON
PEADIATRICS (COLORED) 1:00 P.M. TO 3:00 P.M.
DENTAL (COLORED) 8:00 A.M. TO 12:00 NOON
Saturday
ORTHOPEDIC (WHITE & COLORED) 8:00 A.M. TO 11:00 A.M.
(ONLY EMERGENCIES SEEN AFTER CLINIC HOURS & ON SUNDAYS)

-----*Lallie Kemp Charity Hospital*
https://creativecommons.org/publicdomain/zero/1.0

My segregated school, no exception to Jim Crow rule.

But Jim Crow wasn't everything to me.

I also lived in another world of loving family and community.

Good things and good times were in my neighborhood, like....

Good-time **Motown** music on the radio and at a party on a Saturday night

Good fish fries—with tasty hot, fresh fish fried and seasoned just right

Grandma's and Grandpa's house where I was adored

With their attention I was never bored.

—-*Sonny*

Friendly neighbors chatting on the porch in sunny weather

They had good times and lots of laughter when they got together.

High-stepping Reid High School band marching in the street

—-*Sonny*

Keeping in step and not missing a beat.

My world was small and segregated, it's true, but I had good and fun things to do, like….

Learning that I was somebody, a child of God, and the **golden rule**

Miss Eva and Miss Maggie taught us children in Sunday school

Singing in Wright's Chapel A.M.E. Zion's church choir—Can I get an amen?

—-Sonny

Sharing juicy secrets with my best friend

Going to Sunday school picnics for fellowship and fun

Catching June bugs and fireflies flashing their lights when daylight was done

Firefly Meadow Grass by Diana Wolfskin via Pixabay
https://pixabay.com
CCO license

Going to family reunions—the home-cooked food was so-o-o good!

Learning new dances with my sister and friends and shaking our booty like you wish you could!

Girls just wanna have fun
Ms. Phoenix

Going with sister Jean and friend Alma Jean to the county fair,

screaming on the rides, eating candy apples and cotton candy, and discovering some **phony** shows there

Helping to decorate the Christmas tree

—-Sonny

Receiving Christmas gifts my loving mama and daddy picked out for me and my sister Jean and little sister and little brother Angela and Sonny, too

Jean and Angela, author's sisters

Mama and Daddy, Mrs. & Mrs. John Clinzo Goode, Sr.

Who Santa Claus was some of us knew!

Playing dodgeball and hopscotch in the road

Jean and me and Alma Jean sliding down a hill on our butts when it snowed

Enjoying a bowl of snow cream Mama made out of vanilla flavor, sugar and snow for us children those many years ago

Watching my favorite shows on the TV: *The Ed Sullivan Show, Alfred Hitchcock Presents, The Twilight Zone, Leave It to Beaver,* and *I Love Lucy*

TV Set 5 ----Machovka
https:openclipart.org/detail/2428/tv-set-5

Walking to school with Jean and our cocker spaniel Sandy who knew the time and the way and came back for us at the end of the school day

Cocker Spaniel ----Public Domain
https://pxhere.com/en/photo/624870

Going blackberry picking with Mama, Jean and the sweet Seigle family next door-- Nature gave us, free for the picking, berries, wild cherries, wild plums, honey locusts and more.

These good things I did and ~~washing dishes~~ riding my bike were some of the things I really did like.

Then another world, a surprise, opened up to me.

I loved and was loved by my family and community, and I found a new love when my town, Lowell, NC, built an integrated library.

In the Jim Crow early nineteen sixties, I had never been in such a **public** place before, with no **color line** to bar the door.

—Sonny

Note: My school library was very small, with a very small collection, limited hours and was likely understaffed and underfunded.

I went in Lowell's public library and couldn't help myself!

Books were gifts upon the shelf.

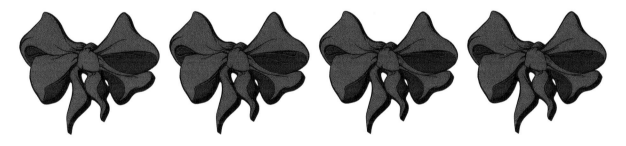

----GDJ-Gordon Dylan Johnson
https:openclipart.org/detail/2366801/red-ribbon

I took books and books took me---up in the air and under the sea.

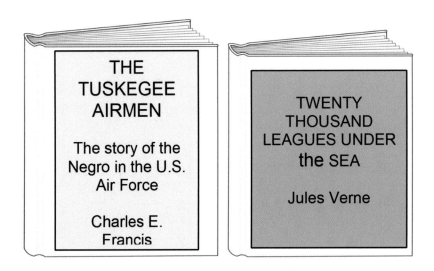

To meet some folks back in history

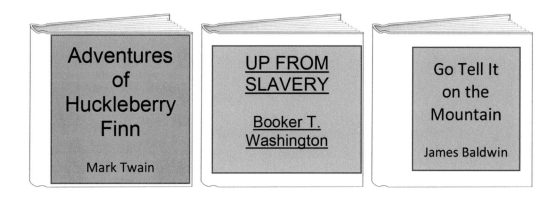

To places far away from me

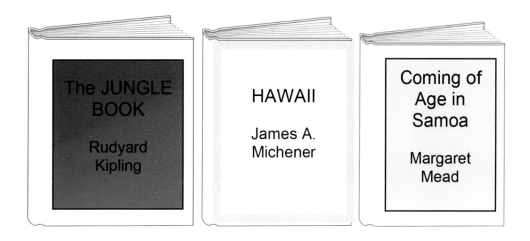

I crossed the border and the track, and that's a fact.

Nothing could hold me back!

With a book as my magic carpet ride, I traveled the world far and wide.

—-Sonny

For me, a small-town colored girl, this door led to a bigger world!

—--*Chrystal Powell Means,*
author's niece

When I got the urge to get away, what did I say?

See yuh!

—*Sonny*

Historical Background of Colored Girl's Entry to Another World----Why She Could Go

When swimming pools, parks, schools, restaurants, and other "public" places and facilities were segregated, the newly built library in my town was integrated most likely because of the **Civil Rights Act of 1964** and the **American Library Bill of Rights of 1961.**

For more information on desegregation in public libraries and the people who fought for the right for all people to use them, go to the websites *The Heroes of Desegregating in Public Libraries* and *The Last Days of Jim Crow in Southern Libraries*.

Glossary

American Library Association Bill of Rights of 1961

"In 1961, it (the American Library Association) adopted an addition to the Library Bill of Rights: "The rights of an individual to the use of a library should not be denied or abridged because of his race, religion, national origins or political views."

----Library Bill of Rights
https://www.ala.org>governingdocs>policymanual

Civil Rights Act of 1964

This act, signed into law by President Lyndon Johnson on July 2, 1964, prohibited discrimination in public places, provided for the integration of schools and other public facilities...............

The act outlawed segregation in businesses such as theaters, restaurants, and hotels...... and ended segregation in public places such as swimming pools, libraries, and public schools.

----Milestone Documents/Civil Rights Act (1964)
https:www.archives.gov>milestone-documents>civil

Color Line

A set of legal barriers that segregates people of color from white people (as by restricting social interaction or requiring separate facilities) and prevents people of color from exercising the same rights and accessing the same opportunities as white people—also called color bar.

----Merriam Webster dictionary
https:www.merriam-webster.com

Five and Dime

A "five and dime" store is a type of small retail store that typically sells a wide variety of inexpensive goods, with a focus on household and personal items. The term "five and dime" refers to the fact that many of the items sold in these stores were priced at five or ten cents.

......https://www.quora.com/What-does-local-five-and-dime-mean

Author's Note: Five and dime stores are no longer in operation. Kress and Woolworth were examples of such stores the author shopped in the nineteen fifties and sixties.

Golden Rule

Rule for how to behave, that you should treat people the way you would like other people to treat you

-----Britannica
https//www.britannica.com

Integrated/Integration

The ending of segregation and allowing whites, African Americans, and all races to be together whether in schools, buses, or movie theaters.

Integration Oklahoma Historical Society
----Okhistory.org

Jim Crow

Just to let you know, Jim Crow got the name from a character in a minstrel show.

"The term Jim Crow originated from the name of a black character from early- and mid-nineteenth century American theater. Crows are black birds, and Crow was the last name of a stock fictional black character, who was almost always played onstage by a white man in wearing blackface makeup. Due to the prevalence of this character, "Jim Crow" became a derogatory (hateful) term for people of African descent."

*----https://www.khanacademy.org/humanities/us- history/
the-gilded-age/south-after-civil-war/a/jim-crow*

"Jim Crow laws were laws created …. to enforce racial segregation across the South from the 1870s through the 1960s. Under the Jim Crow system, "whites only" and "colored" signs proliferated across the South at water fountains, restrooms, bus waiting areas, movie theaters, swimming pools, and public schools. Under Jim Crow laws states could authorize separate facilities not only for schools but for hospitals and clinics, sports events, restaurants, barbershops, railroad and bus stations, restrooms, beaches, public parks, and many other places. These laws were established to enforce racial segregation. Racial segregation is "the practice of restricting people to certain circumscribed areas of residence or to separate institutions (e.g., schools, churches) and facilities (parks, playgrounds, restaurants, restrooms) on the basis of race or alleged race."

----Britannica Online
http:www.britannica.com

Motown

Music released on or reminiscent of the US record label Tamla Motown. The first Black-owned record company in the US, Tamla Motown was founded in Detroit in 1959 by Berry Gordy, and was important in popularizing soul music, producing artists such as the Supremes, Stevie Wonder, and Marvin Gaye.

Phony

Represented as real but actually false

----Cambridge Dictionary
https://dictionary.cambridge.org

Author's note: In the story, the "phony" show was not real or what the people at the fair showing it said it was.

Public

All the people of an area, country

----Merriam-Webster
https://www.merriam-webster.com

Author's note: In the story, "public" refers to a place or event that was supposed to include everybody, black, white or other

Segregated/Segregation

To separate or set apart from others or from the general mass : isolate. 2 : to cause or

force the separation of (as from the rest of society)

---- Merriam-Webster
https://www.merriam-webster.com

Triple

Consisting of or involving three parts, things or people

OED Oxford English Dictionary
https:www.oed.com

Commentaries: Colored Girls Remember

L. Seigle

I probably was about eleven or twelve years old when I visited the library. Going to the library was a meaningful experience for me especially during the Jim Crow era. It was like getting my driver's license for the first time. Now that I think about it, I felt validated.

James Baldwin's books were some the ones that pulled me in. I remember reading *Go Tell it on the Mountain.* It grabbed my attention probably because of the song by that title we sang in church. I also enjoyed reading *Little Women* by Louisa May Alcott. It was one of my favorites. I guess it was fitting at the time because it wasn't so much about skin color but the role of women.

Ralph Waldo Emerson, Mark Twain and Thoreau were some of the authors' names I was introduced to in my school textbooks. I wanted to know more about them and their works.

The library staff challenged us children to read a certain number of books, especially over the summer, and we received stars for reaching our goals. I was always motivated to receive my star for reading a certain number of books. As a result of reading books, I became a better reader and speller, which helped me in my schoolwork.

The library offered doors of opportunity to those who took advantage of it. It took us places we thought we would never go. Through books, we gained knowledge and could see the world through our imagination.

Author's note: Passing the book: As a library patron in childhood, Ms. Seigle experienced the joy and benefits of reading books. As an adult, she helped children discover the world of books. In an outreach program at her church designed to help students who had been suspended from school with their academics, she introduced them to books in her church's library. Some of these students had been bullied and made fun of at school because of their inability to read or to read well. Ms.Seigle engaged them in fun and competitive activities using vocabulary words from books they were assigned to read. Her book reading assignments were well accepted and appreciated by the students.

Wilma Ann Worthy

Swoosh! the sound the door of the library made when opened allowing us to come in out of the sweltering heat. Immediately you were engulfed in the chilling coolness and quietness that seemed irreverent to break.

SHHH! the whisper from Mrs. Isbill warned us to be quiet while nodding her head and pursing her lips to remind us that it was a privilege for us to be there.

Sniff, sniff! The smell of disinfectant, leather and paper. The library was always clean and peaceful. It became my wonderland as I tiptoed between the stacks of books not wanting to draw Mrs. Isbill's ire and be banned from the best place in the world, particularly on a hot summer day.

Aww, aww! The big display window near the front entrance. The many wonderful scenes of places, holidays, and things I'd never seen before were on display to gawk at and marvel over. How much time, patience and imagination that must have gone into those creations. How we envied Edith Edleman. She was a kid just like us, only white, and she got to help out with the displays and other chores around the library.

I was introduced to the public library the summer of my fifth-grade year in school. It was shocking to me that there was such a place that would allow me to look at their books and even bring them home if I hadn't finished what I'd started reading while sitting in the library.

LJ564-- the number on the small manila card that allowed me to take the books home. It fit perfectly in my pocket or the sleeve in the back of the book for safe keeping. It was more precious to me than anything I possessed at this point in my life.

I read all the time, visiting the library two or three times a week or rushing to get there before noon closing on Saturdays. Laura Ingalls Wilder was one of my favorites. I read her series several times. Louisa May Alcott, The Boxcar Kids, Dr. Seuss, Victoria Holt, nineteenth century novels my appetite for reading was insatiable. My reading grew in phases from children's literature to historical fiction, books about French and British history and monarchs, books about espionage and counterintelligence, to informational books. Sometimes I would get in trouble for reading in class rather than paying attention to the lesson. It was at the library that I learned that Lorna Doone was more than a cookie.

I appreciate the public library and how it enhanced by life growing up in the Jim Crow south. Its impact on my life and memories is incalculable. Many years later I've had the opportunity to serve as Branch Supervisor at the Erwin Center Branch of Gaston County Public Library. I consider it an honor and one of my greatest achievements.

The author

I owe the thoughtful and caring librarian Mrs. Margaret Reid Isbill for introducing many patrons like me to classics we may not have otherwise known about. She put classics on prominent display cases near the entry of the library. One of those classics was the first autobiography I read about a black person—Ethel Waters' *His Eye is on the Sparrow.* I shared this book with a friend and a classmate, who shared it with others. I returned the book to the library overdue in a bedraggled condition but was not charged for the fine and damage, probably because Mrs. Isbill knew I was a poor girl who didn't have the money.

Regularly, I would go into my room, sit down with a book and experience magic. With my passport, I traveled outside my room and my town to other worlds and times for adventure and fellowship with people like and unlike me. Reading for me was not only entertaining but also educational, helping me to become a good student by increasing my vocabulary---I kept a dictionary on hand to look up words I was unfamiliar with. Reading also increased my comprehension skills. Reading gave me knowledge of various topics and background information on them. Reading also broadened my perspective. I learned about a wider world outside my own.

My enriching library experiences as a young girl at the public library in Lowell, North Carolina, influenced me to become a librarian. I am now retired after serving as a business and reference librarian at the C.G. O'Kelly at Winston-Salem State Library in Winston-Salem, North Carolina.

Printed in the United States
by Baker & Taylor Publisher Services